DISNEP
PIRATES of the CARIBBEAN
JACK SPARROW

Poseidon's Peak

by Rob Kidd
Illustrated by Jean-Paul Orpinas

Based on the earlier life of the character, Jack Sparrow,
created for the theatrical motion picture,
"Pirates of the Caribbean: The Curse of the Black Pearl"
Screen Story by Ted Elliott & Terry Rossio and Stuart Beattie and Jay Wolpert,
Screenplay by Ted Elliott & Terry Rossio,
and characters created for the theatrical motion pictures
"Pirates of the Caribbean: Dead Man's Chest" and
"Pirates of the Caribbean: At World's End"
written by Ted Elliott & Terry Rossio

DISNEP PRESS

New York
An Imprint of Disney Book Group

Special thanks to
Liz Braswell, Rich Thomas, and Ken Becker

Printed in the United States of America

First Edition
1 3 5 7 9 10 8 6 4 2

Library of Congress Catalog Card Number: 2007906287

ISBN 978-1-4231-0456-8

DISNEYPIRATES.COM

Poseidon's Peak

CHAPTER ONE

*I*n the middle of the great blue Caribbean Sea, a lonely little boat made its way slowly across calm water.

There was no name painted on its weather-worn hull.

A pair of oars, old and full of splinters, assisted whoever might be crazy enough to use such a boat.

The lone sailor aboard seemed to fit that description. The way he rambled to himself, anyone who overheard might think he had at least one other mate on board—possibly a whole crew.

"*Tall peak*, they said. 'Tall peak,' indeed. Bloody sea is flat as a johnnycake. Why can't anyone be more precise? Is 'sail thirty degrees south for ten leagues, then make a right' so bloody *hard*?"

The sailor's name was Jack Sparrow. Once, he'd had a crew and a boat that he'd believed to be a ship. But now he found himself all but lost at sea.

Alone.

The skiff glided past a string of small, beautiful islands. They were covered in dense, green jungle and populated by exotic, brightly colored birds. But they completely lacked anything like a mountain or peak or even a hill—and they grew smaller and smaller as Jack sailed on. At the very end of the archipelago was one particularly tiny

island, about the size of a boulder. A single albatross perched on it. The one bird was about all the rock had room for.

Jack rolled his eyes. Not two days ago, he had been given a tip by a beautiful woman on a beautiful island. She'd told him that great treasure was to be found somewhere in this vicinity, on an island with a very tall peak. So far, no such peak was forthcoming.

After another hour of pleasantly quiet sailing, a larger silhouette finally began to appear on the horizon. Jack sat up, and kept a firmer grip on the oars. A big island came into view. A *real* island. With valleys. Hills. Dales. Mountains.

Peaks!

"Hmm. Mayhap I'll dock there," Jack said casually, tacking into the wind. He didn't want to act too excited. Fate had a way of figuring out when he was happy about something—and then ruining it. The adventures he'd been through over the previous year had proven that.

"But the *Barnacle* got me through it all," he said, a little sadly. The *Barnacle* was Jack's old boat. It had recently been blown to bits by the Royal Navy.*

"Tatty little rust bucket though she was, she got the job done. She was a fine vessel. With the—" He gestured with his hands, modeling his old ship in the air. "*Two* sails, and the . . ." He mimed opening a door. "*Hold* downstairs, and the . . ." He mimed rowing. Then he realized that while he was reminiscing about his *old* boat, the one he was currently sailing had started to drift the wrong way. He quickly acted to redirect himself.

". . . *and the crew*," he finished, irritated.

*In Vol. 10, *Sins of the Father*

"Here I have to get all the work done myself, and I don't think that's quite fair, do you?" he asked, before remembering he was all alone. His eyes popped open and his nose wrinkled in a scowl.

"Not that I miss them, that crew of mine," he added, seemingly unaffected by the fact that he was talking to himself. "Although Arabella wasn't a bad sort."

Arabella Smith had been Jack's first mate. She had believed her mother was dead, then later discovered she was alive and well, and living a pirate's life. Arabella decided to sail with her mother aboard her ship, the Fleur de la Mort. Jack missed her sometimes. But he never admitted it.

Still reflecting on his crew, Jack looked moodily out over the sea. Then he brightened.

"Well, to Davy Jones's Locker with them.

The lot of them! Look at me, here I am, captain of my own boat, my own destiny!"

He slapped the side and yelped as a particularly large splinter stabbed his hand. As the boat gently drifted onto the sandy shore, Jack leaped out energetically. "Ah, look at this view!" He took a deep breath, gesturing to the beautiful island. "Just look at it! Blue sky, sunny sun, sparkling sea! It's a bright Caribbean day. . . . And it's a brand-new day for Captain Jack Sparrow. I am a free and independent man . . . ahem . . . free and independent *captain!*"

He posed dramatically, one foot up on a rock, the cliffs and peaks behind him, the sea before him. "No boatful of idiots to look after, no . . . *dad** chasing after me—this is the beginning of a whole new life!"

*Jack had a run-in with Teague, the man who raised him, in Vol. 10, *Sins of the Father.*

He laid down, supporting himself on his elbows. A playful, sweet-scented breeze blew. The warm sand comfortably supported his back. The sun beamed down warmly.

"This is the life," he said, smiling.

This was, in fact, more relaxed than he had been at any point in the past year. There was no one as far as the eye could see.

Peaceful and deserted.

A quick snooze on the beach and then a hunt for treasure.

Life just didn't get any better than this.

Of course, life rarely *stayed* good for very long.

"Jack . . . Sparrow . . ." a voice called out scratchily.

Jack squinched his eyes. No. It couldn't be. No. Not *here*.

He wearily turned around to look up the beach, wondering what fate had decided to throw at him this time. How it planned to ruin his perfect moment.

Staggering down the beach toward him was a young man, older than Jack, but not much, bleeding from head to toe. There wasn't a limb or appendage that wasn't gashed or scraped. His clothes were shredded and matted with dirt and dried blood. Dark breeches, a white shirt, an old waistcoat . . . a *sword* . . .

Jack reached for his own sword, instinctually.

The man looked like someone who hadn't quite decided to become a pirate. He was dressed like a pirate, but something in his eyes . . .

Someone fleeing his destiny.

"Jack Sparrow . . ." the man groaned again.

Then he collapsed onto the sand.

CHAPTER TWO

$\mathcal{J}$ack looked at the body on the beach.

The man's jaw slowly fell open, revealing a set of not-too-recently brushed teeth. A fly flew by and landed on his tongue. More flies started landing on his wounds and bloody clothes. A gash on the man's forehead was blue and purple and swollen. His eyes were rolled up into his head.

"Urk," Jack said. Overhead, large black carrion birds began to circle.

"Um," Jack said again, trying to decide what to do.

The man's bloody hand clenched suddenly, then in a very final sort of way, relaxed.

"All right, then . . ." Jack said.

With a disgusted sneer on his face, Jack carefully took a step backward. He waited a moment to see if the man noticed.

Nope. Looked pretty dead to Jack.

Jack turned around and quickly began to tiptoe away, hoping to never again see this man or be any further associated with his weird and dramatic death.

Down on the beach, Jack turned to get into his boat with only a slightly guilty sigh.

But his boat wasn't there.

"What . . . ?"

Then he spied it, gently drifting out to sea. Barely a speck on the horizon. "Oh, come on!" Jack shouted, taking his bandana and throwing it on the ground.

He stamped his feet and surveyed the island. The usual thick, green jungle vegetation. No civilization. No one. A fact he had been celebrating a few moments before. Now all it meant was that he had no boat and no way to *get* a new boat. Even if there was treasure on this island, he'd have no way to get it off.

There was only one thing to do.

Jack stomped back to the body on the beach. He picked up one of its hands, then let it go. It flopped back to the sand with a solid *whump*.

"That's it. He's gone." Jack sighed. "Well, guess it's just me, then."

He turned to look out at the sea, holding a hand to his brow to shield his eyes from the sun. If he squinted, he could just barely still see his little boat. Maybe if he built a raft, or quickly rowed a log out . . . maybe catch the tide . . . catch a prevailing wind . . .

Then a cold, dead set of fingers wrapped themselves around his ankle.

"YEAAAAAAGH!"

Jack leaped straight up into the air, whirling around.

Lying back on the sand, but still gripping Jack's ankle, was the man Jack had thought was dead.

"Not quite dead yet, then, eh?" Jack said bravely, recovering his breath.

The other man just panted and heaved.

Jack sighed, a bit relieved. He'd come back to the man because he knew he couldn't make it off the island alone. A raft wasn't going to just build itself. Treasure wasn't just going to dig itself up out of the ground. This bloody guy might be some use. If he healed.

The man tried to speak, but only a dry whisper and a hacking cough came out. He imploringly reached out his other hand to Jack.

Jack sighed and knelt down. He put his arm under the other man's shoulders and carefully raised him up. Sand stuck wherever there was blood, and his hair was dreaded with scabs and dead flesh. A real mess. Jack tried to hold him away a little, to keep from getting his own clothes mucked up.

"Jack Sparrow . . ." The bloody man managed to groan again.

Jack rolled his eyes. "Yes. Yes. You know my name. What do you want, a blue ribbon? Half the bloody Caribbean knows who I am. But the question remains—who are *you*?"

"I . . . I . . . don't recall . . ." the man said, coughing.

Jack turned the man's face into the sunlight. He tried to see past the wounds and swelling, but it was difficult.

This was a weird situation, even for Jack, who had seen so much. All alone on a deserted island, and the only other person was half-dead and somehow knew who Jack was.

Maybe if Jack got the man cleaned up a bit he'd be able to recognize him.

"All right, here's what we'll do, mate," Jack said brightly. He stood, lifting the man with him, and staggered to the edge of the sea.

When they reached the shore, Jack tossed the man in.

"All you need is a good bath. Get you all cleaned up! Make you feel all shipshape and new. Don't forget your pits, mind."

The man howled in pain, seemingly mustering every last bit of energy he had in order to holler.

"Oh, right," Jack said, remembering that

the Caribbean was a sea . . . full of *salt* water. He put a finger to his lips. "How's that old expression go? 'Like rubbing salt on wounds,' or some such? Sorry about that, mate."

The man sat in the shallow water, dripping, stinging, and miserable. But the shock seemed to have revived him some. He shook his head and wiped the blood out of his eyes. He ran his fingers through his hair. He even patted down his clothes, but they were stained beyond hope.

Underneath the blood and grime, he turned out to be a fairly handsome man. *Maybe* ten years older than Jack, but maybe less than that. Slightly built, with light brown hair. Clean-shaven. Soulful blue-gray eyes, the color of the sea. Nice cheekbones.

Jack didn't recognize him in the slightest.

"Bill collector, maybe?" Jack asked, trying to guess who might know his name and be looking for him, though he'd never seen him before. Jack brushed his hand over his sword. "Angry father of a virtuous daughter? *Cousin?* Or perhaps just some random bloke I found on the sand and then gave a good, sharp dunking to?"

But the man didn't seem angry at all. He just shrugged. In fact, he seemed surprisingly calm and even-tempered considering how Jack had almost drowned him. He should have been chasing Jack deep into the jungle, if he were a normal man.

Clearly, he was *not* a normal man. But meeting crazy folks was nothing new to Jack.

"Can you not at least remember who beat you up, like as such?" he demanded, waving his hand, indicating the now clean, but still oozing, wounds on the man's body.

The other man shook his head slightly. "Weren't a man," he said slowly. "Coral . . .

and rocks underwater . . . barnacles and razor-sharp shells . . ."

Jack nodded. It fit the lacerations on his skin. "Thrown overboard then, were you?"

The man shook his head helplessly. "I cannot remember correctly. The last thing was . . . a dark cavern. No, *glittering!*" His voice grew excited as he remembered. "From torch light. It was . . . gold! Glittering gold and gems, rooms of them. In the caverns."

Jack's eyes widened.

"It was deep inside a mountain . . . or cliffs . . . What was it called . . . ?" The man ran a hand through his hair, trying to remember.

Improbably, Jack's eyes widened further. "Something, er, about a *peak*, maybe?" Jack suggested casually.

"Yes! *POSEIDON'S PEAK!*" the man cried out, slapping his hands together.

"That's it! That's the last place I remember before . . . whatever happened. . . ."

Jack jumped up and down enthusiastically.

"Well, where is it, then, mate?" Jack asked.

"I . . . I do not know . . ." the man said, holding his hand to his brow, closing his eyes, and shaking his head.

Jack frowned, squinting at the man. This treasure upon Poseidon's Peak was sounding suspiciously like the treasure he was looking for. So a near-dead man comes out of nowhere on a deserted island who just happens to know Jack's name . . . and the name of the place where Jack's treasure probably was?

That was way too many coincidences for one sunny Caribbean afternoon.

Jack sized the other man up. The man was breathing heavily, still obviously weak. Not much of a threat. Even with his sword.

"Look, I'll lay it to you straight, mate," Jack said, putting his hand on the man's shoulder. "I don't know you from Adam. And I find it mighty suspicious-seeming that you know me, and you know this place, and I just happen to be here, in this place, and there's no one else for leagues around. So I am just a *little bit* concerned about the fact that you know who I am. And *I* don't know who *you* are. Savvy?"

"I'm sorry," the man said sheepishly. "I wish I could tell you more. All I know is that I needed to find you. . . . It was important that I reach you. I need your help. Or someone needs your help."

"You obviously need *some* sort of help, mate," Jack muttered, watching another fly land on the man's wounds to suck up some blood.

He really wished he wasn't the only person around to *give* help. Not that he wished the man any ill luck. But Jack wasn't the sort of person who just randomly helped someone if he wasn't going to get something out of it.

Although . . . when Jack thought about it, maybe the man could help him. If he indeed came from Poseidon's Peak, and that's where this important treasure was . . . Jack would have the fortune that sunk with the *Barnacle* replenished in no time.

And the faster Jack got the great treasure he so richly deserved, the faster Jack would be able to buy a whole *new* boat. And live off the rest of the loot forever. Then he would *really* be free—from everyone and everything.

"All right, mate, I've decided to offer my very noble help to you in your—er—very sorry predicament," he said glibly, putting out his hand. "But first, we've got to figure out exactly who you are and who else it is what has the honorable pleasure of needing my help."

CHAPTER THREE

Three hours later, Jack still knew nothing about his wounded friend.

He tried all sorts of tricks—in case the man was lying—to get him to "remember."

"Did you have a dog as a child? Childhood pet of some sort? *Parrot*, maybe?"

"I can't . . . I don't . . . remember," the man said, shrugging sadly.

"Best friend. Best mate. Pal from the old country. Pen pal. His name is . . . ?"

The man shrugged.

"Favorite fruit?" Jack asked desperately.

"Bananas?" the man suggested.

"Really?" Jack said, glad they were finally getting somewhere.

"No, not really. I have no idea," the man admitted. "I just thought that sounded good. I'd like a banana right now, actually."

"Well, that's very fitting," Jack muttered, "as I am beginning to think that you yourself, my friend, are more than a little bit bananas!"

Jack kicked at the sand. On top of everything else, it was now getting dark. Far too late to start any adventures looking for caverns of treasure on dangerous, slippery peaks. And while the strange man might not have remembered anything about his past, he did seem to remember how to *do* a few useful things. He helped Jack build a small fire, and found several clams and mussels and other small, slimy things to eat. They skewered them on sticks and roasted them over the fire. Jack couldn't tell if he were just very hungry or if this was in fact the best meal he'd had since visiting the village of his former crewmember, Tumen, on the Mayan coast of the Yucatan.*

Soon, the sky was completely dark, and Jack and his new cohort sat down to rest. The wounded man soon fell asleep. And as soon as he did, Jack jumped into action.

Working quickly, he carefully rummaged through the other man's clothes, trying to find something, *anything* that might give him a clue as to who he was. He found a couple of coins in a pocket (which he kept—after all, Jack was better suited to budgeting funds, he was sure of it!). He found a

*Jack visited Tumen's Mayan village in Vol. 5, *The Age of Bronze.*

handful of broken-up coral and sand in a small satchel (which he tossed). He found a small minnow in another pocket (which he ate).

Nothing, not even a knife or a piece of jewelry.

"No watch with an incredibly convenient inscription," Jack grumbled. "Like, 'To Edward. P. Seafluke—if lost, please return to 100 Oxford Street, London.' Not even a blasted signet ring."

He sighed and flopped down next to the fire again, propping his head up against a log. It was a beautiful night, and not that cold. The stars were out. A warm breeze blew off the ocean. Jack could almost pretend nothing had happened: that he still had his boat, that this weird man who knew Jack's name had never appeared.

Dreaming about what a perfect world it

would be if it weren't for other people, Jack's eyes began to close.

Suddenly he was drifting out to sea.

In a longboat.

With no oars.

Jack frowned his typical "What's going on here?" frown. He grasped the side of the boat to make sure it was real. He got a splinter.

It was still night. But unlike the night of a few minutes ago, there was a giant, full moon, hanging low over the ocean. Only a few stars were able to shine through its brightness.

The sea was very still, the boat barely rocking on the water.

Silence blanketed the sea.

"Hmm," Jack said, raising an eyebrow. He dipped a finger in the water and tasted it. "Salty. Just like the ocean should be," he said, unsure what that proved.

He sat back and thought. The truth was, he didn't know whether or not he was dreaming. It seemed like a dream, but it felt so real. . . .

Then the ocean exploded.

In a foamy, seaweedy maelstrom, a huge leviathan called the Kraken rose up out of the depths with a mighty roar. It was the feared ghost ship captain Davy Jones's pet, and its powerful tentacles were waving against the moon and sky.

Jack stood on the boat, balancing, and reached for his sword.

But the tentacles quickly wrapped themselves around him, pinning him down to the deck. One tentacle slid around his throat and began to tighten.

With a *crack*, the Kraken pulled and broke the longboat in half. The fore and aft ends rose high out of the water. Boards and pieces

of deck flew jaggedly through the air.

The monster pulled Jack down through flotsam and jetsam, dragging him under the ocean.

Jack struggled, one hand tearing at the tentacle around his neck. With the other hand he desperately tried to reach anything sharp—his knife, *anything*. But he was still being dragged further into the deep.

Water began to choke him. Bubbles floated up out of his mouth toward the surface.

He struggled harder, tearing at the tentacle's leaves.

Leaves?

Suddenly Jack realized that it wasn't *tentacles* that were holding him tight, but long, thin . . . vines? He was no longer underwater, he was now *falling* from the sky.

The sun was out. It was a beautiful day. Below, green countryside spread out before him like paradise. No jungle; just trees and meadows and hedges and the occasional cow. Vaporous clouds were falling with him, down, down, down toward the ground. Which was rapidly rushing up, up, up to meet Jack. In a hard, unsurvivable-landing sort of way.

Jack hurtled toward the earth—and then he began to slow down. The vines around his legs jerked back, preventing him from crashing. His nose came perilously close to crushing a small, green worm. Jack and the worm had less than a second to look at each other in surprise and dismay.

Because right before he hit the ground, the vines sprung back, taking Jack with them.

Up he flew, almost weightlessly. He

jogged in the air and waved his hands around a bit, trying to get hold of something. But the vines were now slack.

It didn't matter, though, because something else in the sky distracted him from his flying fate.

Mermaids.

Mermaids were swimming through the sky.

Beautiful, with aquamarine and silvery scales. Long red, blond, and ebony hair flowed through the breeze. They sang and leaped and laughed. Much nicer than the Scaly Tails* he was used to dealing with.

"That's it. I've gone completely bonkers," Jack said, refusing to believe any of this

*Jack's encounters with the mermaids—Scaly Tails, as he calls them—are recorded in Vol. 2, *The Siren Song*, and Vol. 4, *The Sword of Cortés*.

was real. He shook his head, trying to knock some sense into himself.

Then he landed on the ground with a loud *whump*.

(There was no sign of the little green worm.)

"Well, could have been worse," he said, trying to sound reasonable. But it was quite difficult to sound reasonable after being attacked by the Kraken and then flying through the sky with mermaids. He brushed himself off and patted his clothes.

"Where in the Seven Seas did I fall from?" he wondered, and put his hand to his brow to look up at the sky.

"*Oh.*" He gulped.

The sky was the sea.

Literally.

It was as though the whole ocean had turned upside down and hung above the earth. It was bright blue, like on a perfect day. Whitecaps and foam danced on its surface like clouds. It might have fooled the eye into believing it was the sky with scattered cloud cover, if it weren't for the occasional whale and dolphin leaping out of the water.

"All . . . right . . . then . . ." Jack said slowly, forcing himself to look down at the ground again.

He was standing on top of a black mountain. Whistling eerily, a harsh wind blew mist through sharp stones and crags.

"Poseidon's Peak, perhaps?" Jack asked optimistically.

He carefully picked his way through the stones and over the boulders, looking for some sign of a path. Here and there, solitary, stunted pines grew in gnarls against the wind. An icy stream of water trickled down lichen-covered rocks.

Jack stuck his finger into the stream and tasted it.

"Salty," he said, a little surprised. He licked the rest of his finger, anyway.

Part of him—a little, tiny part of him, barely a shadow—wished someone else were there to help him. Arabella, for instance. She would have had some long-winded explanation for everything that just happened. And why a mountain spring would taste like saline.

Then he found something that cheered him up immensely.

A cave. Carved into the side of the mountain—into a wall of solid rock. Carved by *hand*, not by wind and rain. Someone had ventured up this very dangerous peak before him. And spent a lot of time hacking out a chamber. Someone who must have had

something very important—very *valuable*—
to stash away.

Jack rubbed his hands together gleefully.

He hopped into the cave and whistled to
himself.

It was pitch black. But even so, when he
turned a corner he saw things glittering in
the dark. Gold, shiny, glittery things: piles
and piles of coins. Chests of jewels. Baskets
of crowns and scepters.

With a grin, Jack reached down and
picked up one perfect gold doubloon.

The rest of the treasure vanished.

"Oh, come *on* . . ." Jack said, closing his
eyes in frustration.

When he opened his eyes, the entire
cavern was filled with skeletons.

Hundreds of them.

"Must stop doing that. Closing my eyes.
Terrible things happen when the lights are

out, as it were," Jack said uneasily. He gripped the doubloon tightly and took a step backward.

He turned to run.

A skeleton fell from the ceiling, onto his shoulders.

Jack yelped.

The sound of a hundred thousand chattering teeth filled the cavern. Bony arms reached up from the floor and out from the walls.

A cold, bony hand gripped his arm.

"*Billy* . . ." it groaned.

"Aaaaaah!" Jack screamed. . . .

And then he saw that the sun had risen. He *had* been dreaming!

He was back on the beach. The sand was cold and damp beneath him. Tiny wavelets lapped at the shore. Everything was perfectly normal.

Except for the still-wounded man grabbing his arm and shouting like a mad drunk from the Faithful Bride inn.

"Billy!" he shouted again. "*My name is Billy!*"

CHAPTER FOUR

"Well . . . Billy it is, then," Jack said, recovering himself. He carefully removed the man's hand from his arm and dusted himself off.

"But Billy is no name for a sailor. I recently met a pirate—a fellow named Renegade Robbie.* You'll be needing a proper pirate name, too, of course. Like . . . *Bloody* Billy. You *are* a pirate, aren't you?"

*In Vol. 10, *Sins of the Father.*

Jack looked at him slyly.

"I don't know," Billy said painfully.

Jack sighed. There was just no tricking him into revealing his past. He really, *really* didn't remember.

"How did your name come back to you, mate?" Jack asked, trying not to show his disappointment at not having uncovered more information. He poked at the embers of the fire with a stick, looking to see if there were any cooked sea snails left.

Billy was silent for a moment. He wrapped his arms around his legs and stared into space.

"It was like . . . I was coming out of a fog, or a mist . . ." he said dreamily.

Jack cocked an eyebrow. It didn't seem like Bloody Billy had emerged from anything at all. He was really too soft-spoken and starry-eyed to be a pirate. He was, however, downright weird. Not the sort of person you would expect to be thrown out of a ship and turn up alive on a deserted island suffering amnesia from said traumatic experience. He was more like the sort of person you would find on a lonely beach staring out to sea.

"Maybe even writing *poetry*," Jack muttered.

"What's that?" Billy asked.

"Nothing, nothing, just a cough," Jack said, waving his hand. Hopefully, all Bloody Billy's strange behavior was just a result of whatever ordeal he had just been through. Knocked on the head, or witnessing something insanely gruesome. Maybe cursed by a sea witch. "Look, you still don't know who we're—excuse me, who *I'm*—supposed to be saving, do you?"

Billy shook his head in dismay.

"Well, here's what we do know." Jack ticked the facts off on his fingers. "One. You have no boat."

Billy looked like he was about to question how Jack knew that.

Jack rolled his eyes and pointed toward the ocean. There were no boats. Not even his stupid little dinghy.

"Unless you've got an invisible one up your sleeve somewhere," Jack added.

"An invisible boat? What an extraordinary idea," Billy said with wonder.

"Oh, yes. Bloody useful, too. I knew a woman once, a raving lunatic of a woman, in fact. . . .* Look, never mind. Long story. Back to the present here, Billy."

Jack took a deep breath and stuck out his fingers again.

*Jack is talking about Captain Laura Smith, whom we first met in Vol. 5, *The Age of Bronze*.

"Two. You remember actually being on Poseidon's Peak. Which, we have to assume, happened before you were thrown into the ocean somehow. What with the cuts and lacerations and fish in your pocket and all."

"Fish in my pocket?" Billy asked, confused.

"Unimportant. It's gone now."

Jack hit his chest and stifled a burp.

"Three," Jack continued, "There are no *peaks* in the general area apart from that one behind us. And by the general area I mean dozens of leagues around. Savvy? I know. I sailed past all the pathetic little excuses for islands around here, including the tiny one that a big bird was using for a latrine."

"But if you sailed here, where is *your* boat?" Billy asked.

"Oh, suddenly you're Bloody Billy, bloody pirate genius, are you?" Jack said in exasperation. "Bloody inspector-general detective doing all the observation and deductions now, are we? Why don't you shut your fish trap for a moment and let me finish. So *three*, noted lack of peaks other than the one formerly stated: there." Jack pointed to the black mountain in the middle of the island. "So, it logically follows that the ominous-looking piece of rock there is none other than *Poseidon's Peak*, what with your recently having been on it, and the lack of other peak-age around here. So we should head *there*. Savvy?"

Billy blinked a little, but didn't disagree.

Two hours later, they were trudging uphill through the jungle. Jack was experiencing a strange sense of déjà vu, as if he had done this all before.

Of course it was because he *had* done all this before. In practically every blasted adventure he had experienced there had been jungle, and sun, and insects, and more jungle, and more trudging through said jungle. If he didn't find treasure *this* time, he was headed someplace cool and flat. Quebec City, maybe. Or the Outer Hebrides.

"Look, why don't you step backward, mentally-like," Jack suggested to Bloody Billy. "Try to walk back through what happened to you. How you wound up on this island, for instance."

"I really can't seem to, Jack . . ." Billy said, panting harder and putting a hand to his side. Jack wasn't sure if this was because he was still injured or if he were out of breath from the hike.

"It would just . . ." Jack sighed. "It would just make everything *ever* so much easier. When we get to Poseidon's Peak, I mean. We'd know how to get in to any secret passageway we might encounter, what to expect once we're in there, where precisely this great and very valuable treasure is. . . . How many skeletons we have to fight off—"

"Skeletons?" Billy asked.

"Oh, nothing, forget that last part," Jack said. "You still can't remember *anything*—not even about your mum and da?"

"Not a thing, Jack," Billy said sorrowfully.

"Well, let me tell you a little bit about *me*, then," Jack said cheerfully. He loved talking about himself. "It's quite fascinating, and maybe it will jog your own memory.

"About a year ago, I'd had it up to my nostrils with the old family back home. Sick of them and the whole family business. Didn't know what I wanted for myself—you know—needed to do a little examination of ye ol' soul.

"I commandeered a boat away from the

Royal Navy. A great ship, called the *Barnacle*. Did it all by myself, too. Then I figured it would be nice to have a crew around. You know, to order about and whatnot. They did a right-fine job of keeping a ship as majestic and grand as the *Barnacle* in order. . . ."

"Crew . . . ?" Billy said strangely.

"Yes, crew," Jack said, annoyed at being interrupted. "There was this wonderful first mate, lovely girl. With surprisingly strong ankles. Could haul a rope like no one's business. And Fitzy—well, dear old Fitzy turned out to *not* be such a loyal member of my crew. . . ."*

"Crew . . . crew . . ." Billy said, thinking.

"Yes, crew, crew, *crew!*" Jack said, exasperated again.

"A ship . . ." Billy said slowly.

* For details on Fitzwilliam P. Dalton III, read Vol. 9, *Dance of the Hours* and Vol. 10, *Sins of the Father*.

"Yes, a crew does usually operate aboard a ship. And, hold your heart, lad, don't want any cardiac stoppage here—one plus one equals . . . gasp, *two!*" Jack said.

"A boat . . ." Billy added.

"Yes, a boat can have a crew, too. And a captain!" Jack said. Then, growing unreasonably enraged, he shouted, "And I defy anyone present or otherwise to say that it can't!" Perhaps Jack wasn't so convinced that the *Barnacle* had been a ship, after all.

"The crew," Billy tried again, thinking hard, "they were looking for a treasure."

Jack's eyes popped open.

Someone *else* was looking for *his* treasure?

"Whose crew? What crew?" Jack demanded. "Are they pirates?"

"Oh, yes," Billy said, staring into the distance. "They are pirates. I'm certain of it."

"Well, then let's double-time it, mate!"

Jack said, marching faster. "We'd best get to the Peak before this nasty crew of pirates gets there and gets all the treasure."

He cast a worried eye up at the mountain. They were only halfway there. And while there was no *sign* of a treacherous, treasure-hungry pirate crew climbing their way to the top, Jack had a feeling that it was only a matter of time. . . .

Another hour of hard hiking brought them above the tree line. It was slow going because the only paths were along game trails—and the game on this island seemed to be quite small: rabbits or tiny pigs or something that only made four-inch walk-ways.

They stopped to survey the peak. Jack took a deep breath and sighed contently.

Billy looked like he was going to throw up.

He was bent over, breathing raggedly. Streams of sweat were running down his face. His puffy eye was even more swollen now.

"Well, look at that," Jack said, pushing aside a strangely familiar, stunted bush. Nestled at the base of two crags was a small temple. What it lacked in size it made up for in decoration, ornately carved with icons of winged gods and butterflies and skulls.

"Well, that wasn't so difficult!" Jack said with a grin. "And not a pirate to be seen! Luck is finally with Jack Sparrow! Let me just go in first, have a look around—"

But before Jack could finish his thought, he was knocked over the head with something hard, and everything went blank.

CHAPTER FIVE

*J*ack groggily blinked his eyes open. Oooh, that was going to be a bad one. He didn't bother trying to feel where he had been hit. He already knew, from far too much experience, that he wouldn't be able to move his arms.

He'd been tied up.

In front of him, like a big tease, was the temple—the ornately carved one that might hold the loveliest treasure in the world. It was so close he could *spit* upon the door from where he sat.

Jack kicked his feet in frustration.

He was answered by a singularly terrible-sounding groan.

He blinked at the ground in confusion.

He tried kicking again. Another groan.

"Ah," he said, realizing he was actually kicking someone else.

Bloody Billy was tied up near him but lying on his side as if he had toppled over at some point. The wound over his eye had cracked open again, and he was also bleeding from some of the scratches on his arms.

"Bloody Billy, indeed. Yech," Jack said.

There was a crunching of stones and pebbles. Twelve pairs of bare feet—and the occasional foot in sandals—marched up in front of Jack.

He looked up. Twelve annoyed-looking

men, brandishing spears, stared at him.
They wore feathers and bright red loincloths
and were amazingly tanned.

"Ah. The friendly natives," Jack said. "I
was wondering when you all would show
up."

One of the men delicately poked Billy's
face with the tip of a spear, to wake him up.

Billy twitched his neck and tried to go
back to sleep.

Jack gave a delicate cough.

Billy's eyes opened a little. Then they
popped all the way open when he saw the
spear point inches from his nose.

One man stepped forward angrily. He wore
a collar of stone beads and more feathers in
his hair than the others. Obviously the
leader or a priest. He barked something—
probably unpleasant—at Jack. He spoke in
a foreign language with a lot of words

that sounded as if something were being swallowed in the back of his throat.

Jack squinted, trying to pick up something from their conversation. He couldn't understand a single word. All his time spent with Tumen, who was Mayan, was bloody useless. But of course, these people might not even be speaking a language that was at all similar to Tumen's.

"Ah, I believe he's saying he's the leader of this village," Billy said.

Jack looked at him in surprise. And Billy looked just as surprised that he could understand the strange language.

"We've trespassed on their mountain and their sacred site without . . . ah . . . asking permission," he continued.

"We need permission to climb a blasted mountain and look for treasure? What is this world coming to?" Jack declared.

The leader, seeing Billy translate, continued speaking. He spoke slowly now and louder, as if that would help the stupid foreigners understand. "He . . . challenges . . . one of us . . . to a duel . . . for our freedom. . . ."

Jack perked up. "Challenge" was good. "Duel" was good, too. And "freedom" was even better.

"If we win . . . we are free to go . . . if we *lose*, we . . . ah . . . must remain slaves until such time as our masters die."

"Well then, who are our masters?" Jack asked brightly. "Probably a pair of old folk, who need help around the house or in the fields. Opening jars, things like that. They'll be dead sooner than you can say 'die.' Nothing to worry about, Bloody, my friend."

The village chief stood aside.

A pair of children, a boy and a girl, six years old at most, stepped forward. They had long, black hair and serious eyes. Their arms were crossed.

"Ah, I believe these two are the masters in question, Jack," Billy said regretfully.

Jack's eyes bugged out of his head. "*They're* our masters? Until they die?" he yelped.

The girl said something sternly, pointing at Jack.

"She says you look untrustworthy," Billy translated. "But you have nice hair. Like a girl's."

"You know," Jack said snippily, "it is *incredibly* convenient you can't remember a blasted thing about your past—or the fact that dangerous natives are guarding the treasure you were so excited about—but you have *no issue at all* speaking some obscure language maybe only five hundred people in the world know about!"

Billy shrugged. "I can't tell you why some things have been lost to my memory and not others."

"Excuses," Jack said grumpily.

The leader of the islanders grew impatient and demanded something.

Billy responded and held out his hands.

One of the other warriors came forward and cut through the vines that bound them.

Then they handed Billy a spear.

"Now wait just a blasted moment," Jack said, not liking what he was seeing. "What in the name of all that's holy—not to mention all the things that aren't—is going on here?"

"I have offered myself to be the one who engages in battle," Billy said flatly. "Since I am the one who got us into this conundrum, I'll get us out of it."

"The bloody bones you will," Jack snorted.

"Look at you—you're a mess! You can hardly see out of your left eye, and your sword arm is so chopped up it looks like the waste room in a tackle shop."

"How did you know this was my sword arm?" Billy asked in wonder, gripping his right hand.

"I didn't. They're *both* chopped up like a plate of bait," Jack said impatiently. "I'm not going to risk eternal servitude to a six-year-old brat—" The girl frowned at him condescendingly, as if she could understand, but Jack kept on going. ". . . because some man who has nearly drowned, been pulled over razor-sharp coral, and sucked at by remoras is getting all noble on me!"

"I'm sorry, Jack, but it is my duty," Billy responded stubbornly. "It's my fault. And I'm the older man. More experience in these sorts of things."

"Well, I *do* admire the ethics of your self-sacrifice," Jack said sarcastically. "In my view, anyone who volunteers himself for potential damage is a blazing lunatic. But *I've* often found in times like this it's better to be pragmatic than noble. And pragmatism would tend to dictate that a *younger* man fight the good fight. If you know what I mean. Younger, faster, quicker . . . fewer bloody wounds . . . can remember my own last name . . . senility not set in yet . . . no troubles recalling *how* I got to this island or *who* my crew is or *where* any pirates looking for treasure in the vicinity might be, savvy?"

Billy sighed, looking at the spear in his hand sadly.

"If you're really insisting," Billy said softly.

"It's for my own neck, mind you, not out of the goodness of my heart," Jack pointed out. "Now tell them to untie me!"

Billy hung his head and said something to the leader. The leader shrugged, then gestured to his warriors. They took the spear from Billy and tied him up again. Then they untied Jack and handed him the same spear.

But Jack's hands immediately flew to his hips. Unsurprisingly, they had taken his sword. Unfortunately, they also seemed to have taken the two or three knives he had hidden elsewhere on his body.

The leader said something to Billy.

"They have taken away our weapons, but they will be returned at the end of the challenge . . . if we win," Billy explained.

Jack frowned. Not only did he love his sword, but right now, more than ever, he needed it.

"If we lose," Billy went on, "we will be tortured with them."

Jack's eyes bulged. He tried not to imagine what sort of creative things an entire tribe— and one very mean-looking six-year-old girl—could do with three knives and a sword.

"Well, I guess this will do," he said bravely, shaking the spear.

The warriors backed off into a circle, surrounding the leader and Jack. The leader took off his collar of beads and a few of his feathers, handing them to the young boy who would be Jack's master. Someone handed the leader a spear. The leader's spear looked as primitive as Jack's: just a piece of sharpened wood. Then one of the warriors let out a fierce cry and the battle began.

The leader of the tribe held the spear over his shoulder with one hand, using the other to steady it. He planted his feet and eyed Jack.

Jack held the spear as if it were a sword,

which was the only weapon he ever really learned how to use.

He gripped it in his right hand, slashing it back and forth in the air like a foil.

Billy closed his eyes and groaned. But not in pain this time. More like hopelessness.

"Take that," Jack said, dancing ridiculously from foot to foot.

The other man spun and thrust his spear.

Jack barely leaped out of the way in time.

When the leader pulled his spear back, there was a piece of Jack's clothing stuck to the tip.

"Hey," Jack said. But before he could come up with a witty insult, the leader lunged again.

Jack tried to parry it the way he would parry a sword blow, but his light wooden spear was easily knocked away. The warrior's spear point scraped against Jack's thigh, drawing blood.

"Ouch!" Jack hissed, rolling in the dust. He clenched his teeth in pain.

The other man said something and laughed. The rest of his warriors laughed, too.

"Don't bother translating," Jack told Billy. "I get the idea."

The leader had just been playing with him. Now he set his eyes and gripped his spear tighter. This was it. This was serious now.

With a bloodcurdling cry, the other man ran at Jack. Jack also cried out and turned to run toward his opponent. The leader planted his sword in the dust and used it to vault into Jack, knocking him down with his feet. Jack hit the ground hard, teeth jarring inside his head. The leader pulled his spear up in one smooth motion and held it to Jack's neck, planting a foot on his chest.

It looked like it was over. Jack and Billy were going to be slaves to a pair of malicious six-year-olds for the rest of their lives.

Jack took a deep breath and rolled—right in between the other man's legs.

Before he could react, Jack leaped up and stabbed him smack on the rear end.

The leader fell over, eyes popping in pain.

The circle of warriors looked on, shocked.

"All right, not a regulation move, but . . ." Jack said, running over to Billy. He wasn't sure if he had won or not. But he sure wasn't going to waste the opportunity to escape. He untied Billy.

"We should go," Billy said, turning to run.

"Ah, not without the treasure, mate," Jack said, turning back to the temple.

"We really need to get out of here," Billy insisted.

The tribal chief was still howling in pain. The warriors were standing over him, looking at Jack and trying to figure out what to do next.

Jack simply took off toward the temple.

"Wait! Jack! Don't go in there!" Billy begged, running after him. "This place—"

His running galvanized the tribe. As one, the warriors shook their spears and ran after him.

Jack bounded, leaping over rocks and zigzagging wildly, trying to lose them. Billy followed as best he could, considering how wounded he was. The tribe followed *him*, doing a much better job. Still, judging from the tracks in the jungle, they were experienced in hunting nothing more dangerous than bunnies, which somehow made this all a lot less scary to Jack.

After tracing a roundabout way, Jack finally made it to the temple door, and threw himself inside.

It was dark and quiet and free from crazed warriors and their spears.

It was also free of any gold.

"What on the Seven Seas . . . ?" Jack demanded, looking around.

The only thing in the main room (which was also the only room) was a simple stone throne. It was surrounded by offerings of the sweetest-smelling flowers.

And fish.

And on the throne was . . . a cat.

A disgusting, huge, mangy old thing with overgrown claws. Garlands of berries and flowers were draped around her neck.

"*Constance?*" Jack cried.

There was no mistaking Constance. She

was the cat that Jack had sailed with when a Creole sailor named Jean was part of his crew. Jean always insisted that Constance was really his sister, mystically transformed into a cat by the soothsayer Tia Dalma. Jack had not seen her since Jean, Jean's best friend Tumen, and the cat had all set off for the Yucatán aboard Arabella's mother's ship, the *Fleur de la Mort*.*

The cat on the throne mewed happily, then began to purr.

It was a purr that sounded satisfied in its grumpiness.

Yep, it was Constance all right.

*Back in Vol. 7, *City of Gold*.

CHAPTER SIX

Constance gave a yowl and leaped into Jack's arms.

"Ew," he said.

She meowed affectionately and began purring, rubbing her greasy head all over Jack and licking at his elbows.

"E-*eewwwww*," Jack said, trying to throw the cat back onto the throne.

With a particularly heavy *thump*, she landed on the floor. But she didn't seem to mind. She immediately picked herself up and began rubbing against Jack's legs, leaving fur and dandruff on his boots.

"Why can't I ever relinquish myself of certain horrible things in my life?" Jack said disgustedly.

Billy was behind him, inside the temple now, watching in wonder. The tribe also filed in—a bit more slowly and respectfully. Two of them were carrying the leader, who was still crumpled over in pain. One of them shouted something at Jack, feebly pointing toward the cat.

"He says how dare you enter the lair of the sacred feline so disrespectfully," Billy said. It was obvious from the look on Billy's face that he couldn't quite believe there was anything sacred about Constance.

The warriors advanced on Jack, spears raised.

Constance hissed and raised a single paw, claws extended.

The tribe immediately backed away, looking terrified.

"She's miserable and gross," Jack said to them, "but not *that* kind of terrifying. I'm sure you all have dealt with far worse in the jungle, what with killer jackrabbits prowling around." Even so, Jack stepped behind Constance, so she was between him and the warriors.

"I think they *worship* her, Jack," Billy said.

"I suspect they're only afraid they will contract some *disease* from her," Jack grumbled. "I was ever so happy to be rid of her." Constance was making him think about his old crew. Not that he missed them. He didn't. The thought of them was just . . . irritating. . . .

And speaking of things being absent . . .

"Where's all the gold, Bloody-Useless Billy?" Jack demanded, rounding on the pirate. "Where are the doubloons and necklaces and crowns and skeletons?"

"Skeletons?" Billy asked, confused for the second time that day.

"Oh, never mind—the big matter at hand here is the treasure. Where is it, mate?" Jack asked, waving his hands about in the air.

"I was trying to tell you, but you wouldn't listen," Billy said patiently. "This place . . . this *peak*, doesn't look familiar. At all."

"This—coming from someone who can't even remember how many toes he has!" Jack said.

"Thirteen?" Billy asked.

Jack rolled his eyes. "And what's your last name again? Oh, excuse me, *I forgot*. You have no bloody idea."

"Look, I tell you earnestly, this doesn't feel right," Billy protested.

"You couldn't have *felt* the not-rightness on the five-hour hike up here?" Jack demanded. "Maybe *before* the friendly natives captured us and I had to reencounter this feeble-minded feline?" he asked, motioning to Constance.

Billy didn't respond, instead turning to the tribe and asking them something in their language. It was all gibberish to Jack, of course.

—except for one word: Poseidon.

He squinted in interest.

The warriors looked back and forth at each other, discussing the question and shaking their heads.

"See, I told you, we've come to the wrong place," Billy said.

"Well. This. Is. Just. Bloody. Great." Jack

said, annoyed—more annoyed than he had been in a very, very long time. In fact, he was annoyed just as much as he had been *happy* on the beach before Billy showed up.

"Here I am, on top of a mountain in the middle of a jungle, inside a treasure-free temple with some weird pirate I don't even know but who knows *me*, and—to top it all off—a cat I really, *really* hate," Jack lamented.

He stomped his foot and threw himself onto the throne. Several of the warriors started to reach out with spears, angered that he had sat there. Constance stopped bathing with her paw and glared at them. They instantly backed down.

"All I have here are more questions," Jack said, really quite put out. "How did *you* get here, for one thing?" he demanded of Constance. "Why is everyone worshipping you? And where are Jean and Tumen? Weren't the three of you traveling to the Yucatán together to spend the rest of your lives lying about on a beach eating bananas or something? We're nowhere *near* the Yucatán. You couldn't *possibly* have *swum* out here by yourself."

He glared at Constance. She seemed to shrug. Her tail whipped up a cloud of dust from the temple floor as it twitched back and forth.

Billy quietly translated for the tribe. They looked vaguely interested.

One tribesman put his hand up and asked a question.

"They want to know who Jean and Tumen are," Billy translated politely.

"Jean and Tumen were a pair of sailors. And *this* . . ." He kicked at Constance. She ignored him. ". . . is their mangy cat, which they insisted on bringing on board. Bloody thing scratched me more times than I can count."

"She looks familiar . . ." Billy said strangely.

"Seen her in your nightmares, maybe?" Jack said distastefully. "No, no, you're thinking of someone, some*thing* else entirely—like a muskrat or a demon from the fifth ring of Hades or something. . . ." Jack sighed with impatience. Turning to Billy, Jack waved his hand at the tribe. "Do something useful for once. Ask these people how she got here!"

Billy translated. One of the warriors answered, with wonder in his eyes.

"Ah, they say she did, ah, swim here," Billy translated.

"*Swim?*" Jack said, disbelieving.

"She just . . . swam ashore. Since cats can't . . . ah . . . swim like that, across the sea, they decided she was a manifestation of a sea goddess. They assumed the sea turned on her and that's why she came to them, wet and cold and shivering. Now they believe it's the tribe's duty to protect her—on this mountain—as far from the sea's wrath as possible."

Jack raised an eyebrow at the warriors. They seemed to shrug.

Billy was staring into space.

"The sea . . ." he began dreamily.

Jack and Constance and the tribe waited for him to finish.

"The ocean . . ." he began again.

"OH, COME ON, OUT WITH IT!!!" Jack finally cried in frustration. He was getting very, *very* tired with his "friend's" way of communicating.

"To get to Poseidon's Peak, we need to travel over the *sea*," Billy explained.

Jack's face lit up. "Finally! Now we're getting somewhere. Let's just hope those other pirates haven't traveled over the sea first."

Jack hopped off the throne and made for the door.

Members of the tribe stepped in. They crossed their spears to block Jack's path. Apparently, interesting stories about crews and cats and sea goddesses aside, they didn't believe he had won the challenge fair and square.

"Maybe if you had explained the rules, *beforehand* . . ." Jack said delicately.

Constance leaped out in front of Jack, getting between him and the warriors, and hissed.

The warriors immediately cleared a path, bowing down to her.

The cat gave a little cough. With her nose

high in the air, she stepped snootily out of the temple.

Jack grinned, his gold tooth shining, and he and Billy followed quickly behind.

CHAPTER SEVEN

$\mathcal{J}$ack, Bloody Billy, and Constance made their way back down to the shore.

Although, Jack mused, it wasn't going to do much good. There was *still* no way off the island.

His own little boat had drifted off to sea. Billy didn't remember how he got onto the island. The natives said that Constance just "washed up" on the shore. Big help that was.

"Maybe there are other villages on the island," Jack suggested hopefully. "With less, er, mountainy natives, and more oceany ones. With ocean things. Such as boats. *Specifically*, boats. Or a smugglers cove. This seems like just the place for one. English and Spaniards and Dutch sailors and pirates or whatnot. Also with boats. As mentioned above."

Billy didn't object. He didn't seem that enthusiastic, either. He just sort of nodded and went along with whatever Jack said, while keeping his dreamy eyes staring out to sea.

Jack figured that if there were any "oceany" settlements on the island—of the smuggler or native type—there would probably be signs of people going to and from the ocean. Signs on the beach. Such as footprints in the sand. Jack marched the three of them around the entire island, keeping his squinting eyes on the shore and the occasional trail into the jungle. Even Constance helped out a little, sniffing out possible paths.

They walked for hours, but they found nothing. Nothing came and went to the ocean except for scuttling crabs and a few sea turtles. And birds. There were a lot of bird tracks, which kept Constance occupied and amused.

"All right, then," Jack said through gritted teeth. The sun hung low in the blue Caribbean sky. "We'll just have to make our *own* boat, then."

"That seems like a good idea," Billy said, sinking heavily to the sand. Although his wounds were slowly healing, he was still exhausted from their crazy day of escaping natives and walking around an entire island. "First thing tomorrow morning, then?"

Jack sneered at this. He was not a morning person.

Constance yawned.

"Aren't cats supposed to be *up* all night, hissing and yowling and keeping people in quiet neighborhoods awake with their demonic sounds?" Jack demanded.

Constance ignored him and folded her paws beneath her chin before settling down for a nap.

"All right, you may do as you wish. I, however, am going to start looking for fallen trees for lumber. And when I assemble a fit vessel, you will not be welcome aboard," Jack said.

Apparently, assembling a ship was exactly what Jack was in the middle of doing when he fell asleep. He woke the next morning uncomfortably draped over a log.

Billy and Constance were peering at him, a little too closely for first thing in the morning. Or, in Constance's case, a little bit too closely for any time at all.

"Hmmph. Wuzzat? Good tree here," Jack said, pretending he was just testing it for strength. He struck the side of it with a weary hand. "Hollow and all."

"It looked like you were asleep there, Jack," Billy said innocently. "We were worried about you. When we woke up, you were gone."

Constance gave Jack a far less innocent look, like she suspected he was up to no good.

"What're you all standin' 'round for then?" Jack said, slurring his words with exhaustion and stifling a yawn. "Go find some logs, too, or we are never getting off this island. Savvy?"

For the next few hours, the three worked as hard as they could to build a raft.

Constance mostly supervised. She meowed when she thought something wasn't being done just right and tested pieces of wood by sharpening her long, yellow claws on them.

Of course, it was difficult to work at all without the right tools. *Any* tools, really.

They could only look for fallen trees, since they didn't have any machetes or axes to cut down live ones. And once they found a usable log, there was no way to cut it down to the same size as the others. Jack's brilliant idea of using vines to tie them all together failed because the only vines they could find were short ones—like those the islanders had bound their hands with. They couldn't get them around the girth of the logs.

After spending an hour trying to burrow through an end log with the tiny knife he used for eating, Jack finally gave up.

"Hopeless," he declared, as if he thought it

had been a stupid idea all along. He even wondered why his colleagues would have encouraged him to do it.

Billy just sighed and stopped pounding his own log, which he'd been beating with an awkward stone.

"*Mrrrow*," Constance said, a strange tone in her kitty voice.

"What's that? What'd you find?" Jack asked with interest. Then he mentally kicked himself for talking to a cat. A cat he hated, no less.

She was a little way into the jungle, sniffing and raising a single paw at something sticking out of the ground.

"*Mrrow*," she said again.

"I think she wants us to go look over there," Billy translated.

"*Really*," Jack said sarcastically. He threw up his hands to the heavens. "Why, oh why, must I be cursed to spend eternity on an island with a creepy-eyed sailor who might be a pirate, and the foulest beast ever to sail the seas? What have *I* done? And the time I took that chest of gold from grandmama doesn't count. After all, it wasn't hers to begin with."

After his rant, Jack stomped over to Constance to take a look. Billy meekly followed.

"Carbuncles and corsets!" Jack said when he saw what she was looking at.

It was part of a wheel sticking up out of the ground. A solid white wheel, with a rim and a few spokes poking out.

He began clawing at the dirt—like a cat.

"Why are you doing that?" Billy asked. "How will a wheel help us—even one as sturdy as this?"

"Because if this *is* part of a carriage or

wagon, it had to get here somehow," Jack explained. "Maybe a ship wrecked here. Maybe a ship with rowboats. Maybe a ship that works and can get us off this bloody island. Failing that, a wagon carriage will be more easily rigged into a raft than some old, dead trees." He imagined with horror what it would look like. Captain Jack Sparrow, standing at the helm of a *carriage*, floating on the water, wheels still attached. Sail made out of a bandana. Billy sitting in the prow, staring out to sea with his dreamy eyes and slack jaw. Constance sitting in a corner, stinking a little.

From the *Barnacle* to the little dinghy to *this*. How, oh, how, had Jack fallen so far? And still no treasure! Or any direction in life, really. It just wasn't fair.

But at least it wasn't a usual wagon.

As he and Billy—with occasional help

from Constance—furiously unearthed the thing, it became clear it was a chariot. Like something out of the days of the Roman Empire. It was little more than a pair of wheels and a platform with three walls, open at the back.

But what a beautiful chariot!

It was light and delicate, made of something creamy white that was neither wood nor metal. Covering the sides were carvings of all sorts of sea things: starfish, barracuda, and monsters—like the Kraken. Details were set off with brilliant aquamarine gems and pearls.

Jack ran his hand over it admiringly.

Then he licked it. Jack nodded.

"Coral. As I suspected. It's made of *coral*," he said in wonder.

"Coral . . ." Billy repeated, running his hand over the chariot in exactly the same way that Jack had. Jack glared at him.

"It doesn't smell," Billy said suddenly.

"What?" Jack demanded, thinking this was finally it. Billy had now completely lost his mind.

"Shouldn't it be all . . . rotten if it was buried here in the dirt for so long?" he asked.

"Humph," Jack said, annoyed he hadn't noticed that himself. It *was* odd. It should have been a little rotted at least—coral didn't last forever if it was exposed to the elements.

Then Jack took out his tiny knife again and began trying to pop out the sea gems that decorated the chariot.

"Jack, stop!" Billy shouted.

"What, you think it's worth more as one piece?" Jack asked thoughtfully.

"I wasn't talking about your thievery, Jack. Look at Constance. . . ."

"I was not stealing . . ." Jack began. Then he turned to see Constance.

She was batting at something on the ground. Something furry, like a mouse buried in sand. But it was too big to be a mouse, and it wasn't moving the way a mouse would, either.

Fearing snakes or something worse, Jack picked up a stick and prodded the ground.

It shook.

Constance began to dig, meowing furiously.

Jack sighed. If the stupid cat wasn't afraid of quaking earth, *he* certainly shouldn't be. He began to dig again and motioned for Billy to do the same. The ground was quivering where the rest of the chariot was still buried. Like something alive had been buried with it.

Jack pushed aside a particularly big skull-like stone and—

There was an explosion of dirt and rocks. Jack and Billy and Constance were thrown several feet away.

When the dust cleared, the entire chariot was standing, free and clear of all debris. And two beautiful horses were struggling in the dirt in front of it, trying to pull themselves out of the hole they were in.

Jack was, for once, at a loss for words.

The horses were still connected to the chariot, and what incredible beasts they were, too. Huge and gleaming blue-black, with blue manes and blue eyes. And very, very strong. It took only a few minutes for them to free themselves. Jack, Billy, and Constance wisely decided to sit quietly out of the way as the horses' razor-sharp hooves dug through the ground.

The horses leaped out onto the ground and shook the dirt from their manes and whinnied in triumph. Sunlight sparkled off their iridescent flanks, and sand and foam blew out of their nostrils.

"All right, then," Jack said, a little bit apprehensive.

The horses looked at him and neighed fiercely.

"Um, are you speaking—neighing, really—to me?" he asked. Without a signal, he and Billy and Constance began to back away from the powerful beasts. They didn't look happy. In fact, Jack assumed they were very angry at having been buried for so long.

The horses tossed their heads, neighed again, and stomped their feet. Their eyes rolled.

Jack, Billy, and Constance backed away faster.

And then the horses took off. With a mighty leap, they sailed over the beach. The chariot arced in the air behind them, landing neatly on the sand. The horses continued running, straight for the sea.

And then into it.

Just a few feet out, they stopped, ankle-deep in the swirling water.

They looked back at Jack.

Now there was no doubt at all about what they wanted.

Jack jumped up and raced toward the carriage. Billy and Constance followed, a little more reluctantly. But as far as Captain Jack Sparrow was concerned, fate had finally given him his just rewards: a way off the island. In a beautiful, elegant craft pulled by two magical horses. It was his just due. He scrambled into the chariot. Billy and Constance pulled themselves in behind him.

"Yah! Yah! Horsies!" Jack called enthusiastically, picking up the reins. He had no idea what to do, really. He was a boat person, not a horse person. "Er, *go!*"

Whether it was from Jack's directions or just the fact that everyone was in the chariot, the horses took off. They ran over the tops of the waves, their hooves churning the water into foam. Their legs blurred: from what little experience Jack had with horses, he knew they didn't usually run this fast, much less on top of water. The chariot glided as if it were on a smooth road, with the occasional bump from going over a swell.

While he was gripping the reins and grinning like a maniac, his two companions weren't faring so well. Billy gripped the sides of the chariot for dear life. Constance was meowing and gagging, lying flat out on the floor, all of her claws dug into the chariot.

"This is the life!" Jack called out happily. "I mean, it's no *Barnacle*—but, really, I won't argue!"

And then the horses dove *under* the water.

Jack cursed his usual bad luck and leaped out of the chariot. Billy and Constance followed. None of them wanted to see if somehow the chariot would afford them the ability to breathe underwater—if it didn't it would be a pretty quick and certain death.

After some desperate swimming, the three of them regrouped.

Constance was completely put out, her wet fur plastered to her body, paws working quickly to keep her afloat. Actually, it looked like she was getting used to being in the water, what with all the practice she'd apparently had recently. She just didn't *like* it.

Jack looked around, squinting and trying to keep his head above the waves. "Over there!"

he shouted, pointing. Then he dog-paddled.

It was his usual, awful, ironic luck: the nearest patch of land was the stupid little rock island sticking out of the water that Jack had scorned on his trip into the archipelago. The one with the albatross poop on it. The albatross was gone now . . . but not its droppings. Sighing in disgust, Jack clambered to the top, which was just a few feet out of the water. Billy and Constance followed.

"This," Jack said, water streaming down his forehead into his eyes. "This," he said again, wiping his face. A fish jumped out of his sleeve. Jack gave up. There seemed to be no words to describe just *what* this situation was. And now, he found a fish in his left boot. Jack sighed and dumped it out, throwing it back into the sea.

"Oh," Billy said, his face lighting up, "I know where we are now."

Jack sighed, closing his eyes. He was very near losing his temper. And he did not want to be accused at some later date of drowning a mentally ill individual.

But still, he was really, really tired of Bloody Billy.

"Oh, yes," Jack said sarcastically. "And where might *that* be?"

"We're up on top of Poseidon's Peak."

CHAPTER EIGHT

*J*ack blinked for a moment, seawater still dripping into his eyes.

Everyone on the little rock was quiet.

"Are you out of your blasted mind?" Jack said calmly. "Oh, excuse me, I forgot," he added. "You *are* out of your blasted mind."

"No, I really am remembering more and more," Billy said, closing his eyes in thought. "Poseidon's Peak is a mountain . . .

that rises from the ocean floor. This is the very top! We're at the . . . um . . . ah . . ." He struggled to remember.

"Peak?" Jack suggested dryly.

"Yes! *Peak!*" Billy said gratefully. "Of Poseidon's Peak. The rest of the mountain is under us."

"Yes, well, here's my problem with your little story," Jack said, leaning forward. "You might remember telling me, oh, not that much earlier in our relationship, that you were there—on Poseidon's Peak. That there was treasure in a cavern *inside* of it. Now tell me, how can that be if it's *under the sea*? Unless there's something else you've forgotten. Like, you're half merman and can breathe underwater."

"It's . . . inside . . ." Billy said, struggling to remember. "*Inside*. There *is* a cave. A cavern. You can breathe. I think . . . I think that's how this happened to me," he said, looking at his scraped and scratched arms. "I was in there."

"A cavern. In a cave. In a mountain under the sea," Jack said, trying to look on the bright side. "If you're right, then at least we don't have to worry about those other pirates finding the treasure first. Now, I don't suppose you remember *how* to get into this magical cavern of treasure, do you?"

"No," Billy said unhappily.

"Of course not," Jack said. "Okay, let's try not to be negative, tankard half full and all that," Jack continued. He tried to mask his impatience behind a teacherlike voice. He pressed his lips together. "Try again. You just remembered where we were—that's very good."

Billy beamed.

"Now," Jack continued, forcing a smile,

"let's try to remember the rest of it. Savvy?"

Billy frowned. He thought very hard. He scratched his temple.

Then he shrugged.

"All right, all right, then," Jack said soothingly. "Maybe you hit your head on a rock or something, and it made you forget. Perhaps we can, you know—reverse the process—clear all the cobwebs."

Bloody Billy looked terrified.

Jack felt around behind him with his hand, until he found a loose stone on the boulder-size island that the three of them were crowded upon and broke it off. "You know, the way a doctor would. By reapplying force to the affected area."

"That only works in stories!" Billy finally protested, guessing what Jack meant to do. He covered his head in fear.

Jack rolled his eyes and tossed the rock

into the sea. "You are not very cooperative," he said in disgust.

"I'm trying, Jack, I *really* am," Billy said with meaning. "I remember the treasure!"

"Treasure?" Jack's eyes lit up.

"It's not gold or jewels or anything like that. . . ."

Jack's face fell.

"It's more powerful than all of that."

Jack's eyes lit up again. "Do go on," he said.

"It's . . . the sea god . . . *Poseidon*," Billy said, trying to explain it simply and not in his usual way of speaking. In case Jack decided to bop him on the head anyway. "It's his trident. It's in a chamber somewhere below us. The trident is very powerful— it's the weapon of a god. It can cause earthquakes, wreck ships, summon the Kraken . . . and, and then . . . then there is the most important part . . ." he said in a whisper.

"More important than wrecking ships and calling down the wrath of the heavens?" Jack asked mockingly.

"It can control the merfolk," Billy said, remembering with an awed hush. "All of them. If you have the trident, you control every merman, mermaid, and merchild on the Seven Seas."

Jack was silent. That *was* really important. Huge, in fact. Whoever had the trident would rule the oceans. He could decide which ships got to sail where. He could force whole countries to pay him ransom to let ships through. He would be free to do whatever he wished—*whenever* he wished.

Constance, slipping a little on the rock, chose that moment to reposition herself and dig in her claws, into Jack's foot, that is.

"OWW!" Jack spluttered, his glorious daydream interrupted.

Constance made a purring sound and looked at him, as if to say, Oops. Sorry I *accidentally* clawed you.

"You *stupid*, useless, *mangy thing!*" Jack cried, forgetting how the cat had just saved them all from the natives. "You like swimming so much? Here's another chance to practice!"

And with that, he picked her up and threw her into the sea.

The cat hissed and desperately flung her paws out, trying to keep her head above the waves.

And then she slipped under.

A trail of bubbles went down, down behind her into the deep.

"Oh," Jack said, horrified. He only meant to scare her, not drown her. She might have been a mangy awful cat thing, but she had also been a member of his crew. And she was possibly Jean's sister.

"Oh, heavens," Billy said in his vague way.

"Blast, blast, blast!" Jack said under his breath. He kicked the rock he was standing upon, which he still didn't believe was really Poseidon's Peak.

Then the water exploded, and a yowling, screaming thing came tearing out of it.

Jack and Billy screamed and grabbed onto each other.

"KRAKEN!" Jack cried.

But it was Constance, leaping back onto the rock behind them.

Jack clutched his chest, where his heart raced wildly. "Don't *do* that."

Constance ignored him. Instead, she ran straight back to the water—and dove in.

A moment later, her wet little head popped up again.

She meowed and pawed at the water.

"You want us to take a swim with you?" Jack asked slowly.

"*Mrrrow!*" Constance said.

Without hesitation, Billy executed a sweeping dive into the ocean.

Jack looked around. Nothing for miles. He was either going to stand here and survive for a day or two, or he could follow the cat and the crazy man, and hope for the best.

Sighing, Jack held his nose and jumped in.

CHAPTER NINE

*I*t took a moment for Jack to adjust to being underwater, but he quickly learned to enjoy it. Down here there was nothing to worry about: no pirates, no insane fathers, no decisions about what to do with his life . . . it was almost like being on that deserted beach again, before Bloody Billy showed up, of course.

But there was no air down here.

At first, his eyes stung when he opened them, and it was hard to focus his sight properly. Everything was blurry. As he kicked, not sure where he was supposed to be swimming, thousands of bubbles floated up, making it even harder to see.

But after a moment, Constance's grizzled face popped up in front of Jack. Her fur was studded with thousands more bubbles. On a prettier cat they might have looked like pearls. On Constance they looked like warts.

With an impatient lash of her tail she spun around, not waiting to see if Jack followed her. Jack shrugged—an awkward movement to make underwater—and swam after her. Billy kept close behind.

Jack hoped the cat knew where she was going and wasn't just trying to get back at him for throwing her into the ocean.

The water got murkier and colder the deeper they dived. Jack tried to avoid the sharp, black rocks that were all around them. Slithering between the rocks were huge, slimy, hoselike creatures, that Jack figured could only be eels of the man-eating variety.

Then Constance disappeared entirely.

Jack closed his eyes. He felt as if he were about to explode, and he kicked to ease the pain in his breathless lungs. Then, unexpectedly, his head popped up out into *air*. He took a deep, gulping breath followed by several shallower ones, acclimating to the sudden abundance of air.

Bloody Billy burst up next to him, choking and spitting out water. Jack clapped him on the back, not paying much attention to his travails. Jack's patting only made Billy choke and cough more.

The cavern they had emerged in was a lot like the one under Isla Sirena,* where the merfolk lived. There was no discernible break in the surface, yet the air was, if

*Jack was there in Vol. 2, *The Siren Song*, and Vol. 4, *The Sword of Cortés*.

not fresh, at least breathable. A strange blue-green light glowed from the roof.

Constance soon pulled herself out of the water and into the chamber, shaking the water off herself and sneezing.

Jack climbed the rocks that ringed the room and took his bandana off to squeeze the water out. He looked at it disgustedly and then put it back on his head. It felt like a dead, wet fish.

"So, what on earth do we do now?" Jack asked.

As the group's eyes grew used to the gloom, the far edges of the chamber came into focus: a dozen or more passages, black and cold, led off in every direction.

"All right, Mr. Half-Remembering Billy," Jack began.

"I thought my name was Bloody Billy. That's what you called me before," Billy said.

Jack rolled his eyes. "Just pay attention, will you? What's behind door number one? Or two? Or three? Or thirteen?"

Billy blinked. "I don't see any doors, Jack. Just caves."

"Does *any* of this look familiar to you?"

Billy thought hard. It was obvious from the way he squinted his gray eyes.

"I don't know, Jack," he finally said, sadly.

Constance sneezed again. Then she took off into one of the caves, quickly disappearing in the darkness.

"Well. That's it for her, then," Jack said, not upset at all. He turned back to Billy. "Now where were we?"

"Maybe we should follow her," Billy suggested hesitantly. "After all, she found *this* place. . . ."

Jack grumbled and frowned at the idea of having to follow Constance. But perhaps Billy had a good point. "Well, the blasted cat-thing *can* see in the dark better than we can, after all," he conceded. "But just so you know, in the future, it's the *captain* who comes up with the good ideas. And not just any captain. This one. Right here. Captain Jack Sparrow."

And with a dignified twirl, he marched after Constance. Only twenty steps in, and the darkness was complete. The tunnel ceiling was just a few inches above Jack's head; Bloody Billy had to stoop. Jack let one hand brush along a wall, to keep his orientation. And he stopped immediately when something slimy moved underneath his fingertips. While the floor was mostly worn smooth, there were treacherous stalagmites here and there, and puddles of ooze and slime. The constant sound of dripping moisture echoed through the cavern. Now and then something slithered wetly in front of—or over—

his feet. And sometimes things—little things, with big teeth—would snap at his boots. Occasionally, their teeth bit right through the leather.

Jack gritted his teeth and pushed on.

Once in a while Constance would meow to let them know she was still there, ahead of them. After what seemed like an eternity of walking in darkness, they emerged into the light . . .

. . . right back in the chamber they had started from.

"Brilliant! We've just walked in a complete circle," Jack said. "I guess this is what I get for listening to a cat and a bloody lunatic."

Billy looked quietly perplexed.

Constance was moving from archway to archway, sniffing carefully at each of the chamber entrances.

Then she darted back through the one they had just emerged from, meowing loudly.

Billy started to follow her.

"Negative," Jack said, putting his hand out to stop him. "No, nay, *nein, non,* and generally not at all. We are *not* following that flea-bitten, mangy furball in a circle again. We're going to strike out on our own. Like the intelligent human beings that we are."

"Jack, that's not fair to Constance," Billy protested. "We have no idea how many twists and turns there were back in there. It was completely dark. Maybe she took the wrong one and is now trying to find the *right* path. We should try again."

"NO," Jack said, marching across the chamber. In a fit of sheer pique, he chose the cave exactly opposite the one they had just come through.

But as soon as he put one foot in, an

unearthly howl reverberated throughout the chamber. It sounded like a cross between a rabid wolf and a bleating cow.

Jack quickly ran back out.

"All right," he said, fixing his bandana. "We'll follow the cat."

Jack ran his hand around the wall. Again. And sometimes he felt teeth biting through his leather boots. Again. Jack gritted his teeth and pushed on. . . . Again. Once in a while Constance would meow to let them know she was still there, ahead of them. Again. When they finally came out . . . it was into the same chamber.

"Again?!" Jack said. "Well, that does it." He skipped over to Constance.

Constance growled and hissed at Jack.

Then she turned and went back into the *same* passageway. *Again!*

Jack was so flabbergasted he could barely

speak. An extremely unusual state for him. He turned to Billy.

But he stopped when noises came from *another* tunnel. Heavy boots clomping. Chains rattling. General piratey noises.

"It must be the pirate crew!" Billy called out. He turned to follow Constance. "We must advance, or they will find the treasure before we do. And who knows what such vicious and terrible pirates could do with such power as is contained in Poseidon's Trident?"

"Sorry, mate. There is *no way* I'm going through there just to come out here again!" Jack protested.

The footsteps came closer. They could hear other noises now—sabers rattling, grumbling voices in guttural tones.

"What should we do, then?" Billy asked, his eyes a bit glazed over.

But before Jack could answer, a bronze gate came crashing down over a cave entrance. And then another one. And another one. Gates were coming down over *all* the passageways from one end of the room to the other, cutting off their escape routes.

Billy ran after Constance.

More gates crashed down.

The footsteps came closer.

Soon there were only two passageways left open: the one Constance and Billy had gone through and the one that led to the pirates.

"So, let's see here," Jack said philosophically. "Run headfirst into a gang of violently angry and armed pirates, or follow that wet, stinking cat in circles again."

He scratched his chin, thinking.

The final two gates began to close.

"Oh, all right," he sighed and dashed after

Constance and Billy.

But the footsteps kept coming—the pirates had followed them into the tunnel.

"*YOU!*" A deep, powerful—and very strong—male voice called out.

"You, who?" Jack called back. "No one here, mate, sorry. Not sure who you're talking to. Must be going mad. Just echoes in here, that's all. 'You . . . ! You . . . ! You . . . !' See?"

He began to run.

Which is why it hurt an awful lot when he slammed into Billy, who stood stock-still at the tunnel's exit.

"Room for your captain, then," Jack said, preparing to push him aside and keep running. But then Jack stopped, too.

They weren't in the same room they'd kept coming back to. They were now in a chamber filled, absolutely *filled*, with artifacts and gewgaws and antiques and treasures and . . . *things*. Egyptian death masks. Tea sets. Greek statues. Pearl necklaces. Silver fountains. Used spittoons. Golden chairs. Jewel-encrusted lanterns. Chests piled high with ancient money. Glass mirrors. Swords. Wooden teeth. Piles of emeralds.

In the middle of the room was a low pool, whose sides were covered with gems and pearls. It was filled with black, viscous water, and in the center was a pure white coral pedestal that looked like it should have been the stand for something really fantastic. But there was nothing there.

Jack's jaw dropped in awe. Even Constance appeared dumbfounded: she stood still, eyes darting from treasure to treasure. She fixed on a jeweled brooch fashioned after a rat.

They were so astounded that they forgot about their pursuers.

Who crashed out of the tunnel and onto them—toppling everyone (and a few treasures) to the ground.

"*Jack?*" a familiar voice said.

"Bell?" Jack asked, replying out of force of habit to a voice that sounded like his former first mate's.

But then . . .

"Constance!" a green-eyed boy said with delight.

"Jean?" Jack asked, unable to believe what he was seeing.

"And Billy! Billy Turner! It really is ye! Ye've made it out alive! Ye found Jack!" Arabella shouted.

"Mister Reece! Jean! Have you apprehended the culprits?" an authoritative female voice demanded. "How they'll rue the day they crossed the crew of the *Fleur de la Mort*! How I'll enjoy making them answer to me . . . Captain Laura Smith!"

"Laura, Laura, Laura—as dramatic as ever," Jack said coolly, picking himself up and dusting himself off. His entire old crew was there—except for Fitzwilliam P. Dalton III.*

And Arabella's mother, Captain Laura Smith, and her dashing first mate, Mr. Reece, were there, too.

"Laura, still as ornery as ever. The months we've spent apart haven't changed you any, I see," Jack said.

"YOU!" Captain Smith shouted, tossing her hair in surprise and anger at seeing Jack.

"Yes," Jack said with a grin. "Me. Now, do you mind telling me how *you* all came to be here and what in the name of Davy Jones's Locker is going on?"

*To find out why Fitzy's not among the reunited crew, be sure to read Vol. 9, *Dance of the Hours*, and Vol. 10, *Sins of the Father*.

CHAPTER TEN

"Stars and saints! I thought ye were dead!" Arabella cried, throwing her arms open.

With a surprised smile, Jack opened his arms and waved as Arabella came running toward him—and then right *past* him, into the arms of Bloody Billy. As Billy and Arabella kissed, Constance coughed up a hairball disgustedly.

"Ahem, begging your pardon," Jack said. He carefully put a hand on each of their shoulders and pried the happy couple apart. "Congratulations on your apparent soul-mate discovery, but it's not something we all need to witness. Savvy?"

"Sorry, Jack," Arabella said with a beautiful grin, her eyes still fixed on Billy. "Can I introduce ye to bosun and third mate of the *Fleur*, Billy Turner."

"Dumb name," Jack said without hesitation. "I'd stick with 'Bloody Billy,' if I were you. Besides, Bell, he doesn't really seem your type—all mushy and, frankly, odd."

"Oh, yer one to talk about 'odd,' Jack!" Arabella said.

"I'm remembering it all now," Billy interrupted, sitting down on a chest of trinkets. "*These* are the pirates who were after the treasure!"

"What, this lot?" Jack asked, jerking his thumb toward Laura. Captain Smith bridled with indignation. "I thought you meant *real* pirates."

"You think just because I'm a woman I cannot be a pirate captain?" Arabella's mom said indignantly.

"No, no," Jack said soothingly. "Absolutely, women can be real pirates. I just meant *you* can't because you're bad-tempered, huffy, very rude, incompetent, and a general blowhard."

Speechless with rage, Captain Smith lunged at him. Mr. Reece held her back. Jack ignored both of them.

"You were saying, Billy? Go on, go on . . ." he prodded.

"The navy . . . picked me up for being a pirate," Billy said, putting a hand to his head. "But I wasn't. I just didn't have the right papers. It was all a horrible, horrible mistake—and then they came across the

Fleur de la Mort and we were attacked. It was a close battle—"

"Nonsense," Captain Smith sniffed.

"—but the good lady here drove them off and rescued me, thinking that I *was* a pirate . . ." Billy looked up at Jack and shrugged. "So I joined them. I tried the honest route and look where it got me. The pirates were far more gentlemanly."

Laura Smith glared at him.

"Er, womanly," Billy quickly corrected.

Mr. Reece glared at him.

"Er, man-and-womanly," Billy said desperately.

"So *you* were one of the pirates that we were racing against to get the treasure," Jack said smugly.

"Unfortunately, yes," Billy said with a wan smile.

"That's just lovely," Jack said, sighing. "So

how did you lot wind up here?"

"We unfurled our sails," Laura Smith picked up where Billy left off, "the mainsail, which makes the *Fleur* invisible. But not before heading further out into the Caribbean—away from the Yucatán—to throw the navy off our trail."

"We were just past Antigua," Arabella said with a sigh, remembering, "when we got caught on a reef."

"Despite being invisible," Billy continued, "we were caught there like lobsters in a trap. We were abducted."

"The navy was able to trace you all that way and catch you—even though you were invisible?" Jack asked, surprised and impressed.

"*Not Man's navy*," came an eerily familiar voice. "*Ussssss.*"

With an oily, liquidy splash, the dark

water in the pool before them rippled. Emerging from the waves were Morveren, Aquila, and Aquala. The three made the head council of the merfolk.

"Oh, not *you* blasted Scaly Tails," Jack groaned.

"We are the appointed keepers of Poseidon's Trident," Morveren said grandly.

"It is a weapon of the gods, with great powers," Aquila hissed. "Poseidon used it to torment us for generations, controlling us—making us do whatever he wished."

Jack had to admit that it must have been pretty funny. Imagine being able to make those merfolk do whatever you wanted! He had visions of a mermaid feeding him sardines while another one juggled cats—and one cat in particular—for his entertainment.

Morveren continued. "Hundreds of years ago, the merfolk finally won the trident away from the god of the seas in a great contest of skill."

"Oh, *that* must have been something to watch," Jack said drily, imagining these tailed creatures attempting to jump through hoops.

The merfolk ignored him.

"We won our freedom. His staff and his chariot became ours. The trident was hidden here, and the chariot is still hidden—buried on an island not far from where we now speak."

"Now someone else has finally found the trident and is capable of complete control of the whole race of merfolk," Aquala said. "And is wreaking havoc upon the Seven Seas."

"Everyone except we three of the Blue Tails," Morveren added, with a *thwack* of her own tail. The incredibly rare race of merfolk was apparently unaffected.

"And this is the part where I . . . care?" Jack said, leaping up into a gilded throne and casually leaning back. "You Scaly Tails have never been a particularly pleasant lot. And you've wreaked havoc on the seas before *without* the excuse of someone else's trident. The only thing I'm sorry about is that *I* didn't find the trident first!"

"We've never upset the balance of the seasssss," Aquala said through gnashed fangs. "Now an entire army of merfolk is amassing, possibly to wage a great war."

"Still not at the part where I care," Jack pointed out.

"Jack!" Arabella admonished him.

He shrugged helplessly.

It was almost like old times.

"*This* is the point where you *should* care," Morveren said sternly. She tossed her glimmering red hair. "We captured the *Fleur* looking for you, since we believed you were the only land dweller clever enough to secure the trident!"

"Really? Me?" Jack said, sitting up. "You think I'm the cleverest person in the world?"

Morveren ignored him. "But your filthy cat escaped. She jumped ship and swam for shore. Horrible beast."

"Well, you and I agree there, at least," Jack said, sighing. "She *is* filthy. But good job, upsetting the half-fish," he added, to Constance, patting her on the head. Constance meowed quietly and purred.

"We brought the rest of the crew for safe-keeping here, under Poseidon's Peak, where we merfolk keep the spoils of all our greatest wars," Aquala continued.

"Greatest wars, huh?" Jack asked, holding up the set of wooden teeth he'd spotted earlier.

"We used our looking-pool, which allowed us to observe the world above," Aquila hissed. "We saw you rowing to the island where the chariot is buried."

"*Was* buried," Jack corrected without thinking.

"What?" Morveren asked.

"Nothing," Jack said quickly. "Please continue with your *fascinating* story."

"We knew you were *our* only hope, when we saw you, Jack," Arabella said. "Jean managed to pick the locks to the cages we were kept in—but we got lost in the tunnels that riddled the mountain."

"Why does everyone want something from me?" Jack mumbled.

"I was sucked up by a waterspout, one of their traps," Billy said, remembering. "It jettisoned me up and out and through the sea—and several reefs of very sharp, very hard coral . . ." he added, rubbing his head and looking at the wounds on his body.

"Ye're not *too* hurt, are ye, Billy?" Arabella asked, laying a concerned hand on Billy's shoulder.

"That explains the . . . ah." Jack made crazy motions.

Billy shivered. "I'd be happy if I never saw another slimy, sharp, nasty sea critter again. But I found you! I found Jack. . . . A lot of good it did us, though. . . ." He finished sadly, looking around the room.

"You must help us, Jack," Morveren demanded. "You and the crew of the *Fleur*."

"Now just hold your sea horses, there, mate," Jack said, finally losing his temper. He leaped off the throne and walked toward the merfolk, grabbing a deadly-looking silver sword from a pile of loot as he went.

The crew of the *Fleur* and his friends

drew back. They had never seen the even-tempered Jack Sparrow so angry before. But it was happening more often since Fitzy turned mutinous and Teague had appeared back in Jack's life.*

"*First* you try to kidnap me to steal something back for you," he growled. "*Then* you *actually* kidnap my old crew, hoping they'd lead you to me. Then after we've all been battered and tossed about by your stupid little fish games, you demand our *help*? After everything you've done?"

"You scaled scalawags!" Captain Smith barked, drawing her own sword and advancing with Jack. "You tailed tarts! Of all the nerve! We should skin you now and have you in a chowder for all you've done!"

"For once, Captain Smith, you and I are in

---

*In Vol. 10, *Sins of the Father*.

agreement," Jack said. "Though I don't really want to think about what mermaid chowder might taste like."

"It's delicious," Laura said with a twisted smile.

"Mother!" Arabella snapped.

"Or so I've *heard*." Laura said quickly.

"Let's just get out of here," Billy suggested. He was obviously done with all of his adventures at sea. Jean, Tumen, and Arabella all nodded in agreement.

Jack looked disgusted. "All right. You've lucked out. We'll just go our way and . . ."

Just then, the cavern began to shake.

Dust fell from the ceiling, along with bits of debris.

Jack was about to accuse the merfolk of more tricks—but they looked just as surprised and terrified as everyone else.

There were several loud cracks that

sounded like thunder. Everything shook.

Large pieces of rock and coral tumbled down from the walls. Shells were crushed into a fine, white powder.

Then, the rattling stopped and dust settled in the watery chamber, which suddenly didn't seem all that stable.

As the dust settled, a figure appeared in silhouette at the center of the pool where the pedestal stood.

A sudden spark filled the room, followed by a series of popping, sizzling electrical noises.

Before the crew was a tall, grimy man. He wore a long, torn overcoat, and his dark black hair hung in front of his eyes, which sparked like lightning. He rode the chariot Jack and Billy had found. In one hand he snapped the silver reins. In the other, he held a giant trident.

And he didn't look happy.

"Oh, my . . . it's Torrents . . . the terrible, awful captain we battled in our first adventure together," Arabella whispered in awe.*

"And he's got an entire mermaid army fighting for him," Billy Turner said.

Jack looked anxious, but determined.

"Like it or not, Grand Mistress Scaly Tail," Jack said grimly to Morveren, "I suppose we're involved in your little war *now*."

To be concluded . . .

*Way back in Vol. 1, *The Coming Storm.*

Don't miss the <u>final</u> volume in the earliest adventures of Jack Sparrow and the crew of the mighty <u>Barnacle</u>!

Bold New Horizons

It's all been building up to this—the *final* volume in the epic chronicle of Jack Sparrow's first year at sea. You won't want to miss it. Savvy?